8/17

This book provided by
www.SuccessWontWait.org
In memory of Karen L. Valone
of the Claymont Public Library

D1406805

A Foal Is Born

Elin Meldahl Ellingsen

Translated by Osa K. Bondhus

Photos and text draft: Elin M. Ellingsen
Rewrite and text adjustments: Eli. B. Toresen, Stabenfeldt AS
Published by Stabenfeldt
Layout: Kristin Eriksen Berg
Editor: Bobbie Chase
ISBN: 1-933343-46-X

Stabenfeldt, Inc.
457 North Main Street
Danbury, CT 06811
www.pony.us

A glimpse of sun appears in the dark sky.
It lights up and creates exciting shades of color in the world around us.
Always treasure the little glimpses of light,
because they are often sources of joy in your life.

Thank you …

I'd like to thank all my good friends, who are there for me when I need a boost.

I thank El Patron for being such a great and gentle horse, a horse with a big heart. It has been a pleasure to tell the story of his life here at the stud farm. I hope he will find a new owner some day, someone who will appreciate his good qualities and wonderful disposition as much as we have.

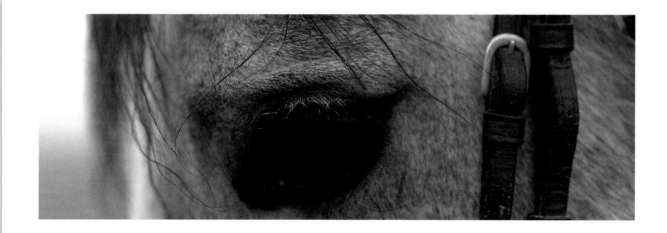

It may be fun to daydream about a life working with horses – and I won't deny the fact that horse breeding is a very exciting, fun and challenging job – but more than anything, it is a lot of hard work. You spend a lot of time feeding, mucking out stalls and making sure the horses get enough fresh air. The fun part, which is training the horses, comes as an added bonus.

At our small stud farm in Norway we do all the work with the horses ourselves. We don't get weekends off, and we can't get up one morning and say we don't feel like working today. The stalls have to be cleaned out every single day, and believe me, it isn't all that exciting when it's wet and cold outside, and the wind blows straw and shavings straight in your face as soon as you open the door to the stable. And there are difficult days, when a horse gets injured, or gets sick, or dies. But there are also wonderful days when the sun is shining from a clear, blue sky, the foals are jumping around playfully, and the mares greet us with their contented snorts. That's the real payback for all the

hard autumn and winter days when we felt like giving up. But what really drives us to keep doing this is, of course, the totally unique contact we have with our beautiful animals.

Few things in life can give more joy than going for a horseback ride, galloping into the wind, and feeling the power of the running horse beneath you. At other times, the joy comes from training in dressage and finally mastering a new technique for the first time. But the best thing of all is to be able to lean into your horse and confide in it all your deepest secrets. It won't tell on you, but just listens quietly. It seems as though your horse can see deep into your soul when it looks at you with its beautiful eyes. It's then that you know you couldn't fool it for a second. Your horse will never think you are anything but the person you really are.

You actually learn an awful lot about yourself by working with horses.

THE DREAM

Who hasn't dreamed about owning a horse, making a mark on it, and having exciting adventures with it? Having a horse from the very beginning, when it's a newborn foal, is no doubt the easiest way to establish that kind of relationship with a horse.

Raising a foal is not easy, however, especially if you don't have a lot of experience with horses beforehand. It is extremely easy to spoil them. If a foal is handled too much, not to mention handled the wrong way, by its owner, it may come to lose its respect for humans, and possibly not learn how it's supposed to behave. This is particularly true for bottle-fed foals (foals who for some reason cannot be with their mothers and therefore have to be bottle fed). Because these foals are not reared by their mothers they don't have the same opportunities as other foals to learn the natural body language of horses and to find their places within the herd. That doesn't mean that these foals can't learn it, because they definitely can. Many of them turn into very good horses eventually, if they are given the right groundwork.

There is always more than one way to reach a specific goal. I'm not claiming that our way of handling foals and young horses is the only right way, but we have found a way that works very well for us. Our horses show trust in humans and are easy to work with. The Arabian horses that we work with are known for forming strong attachments to humans, and that's why we put so much time into our relationships with our horses.

We don't normally have a lot of foals at any given time. But we usually have more than one, which means that raising one becomes a little easier. Personally I don't care much for the idea of a foal growing up at a riding school, nor in a stall by itself, left alone after the separation from its mother. On the other hand, it's not healthy for the foal not to be separated from its mother eventually either. That can lead to the foal becoming so dependent on one particular horse that it causes difficulties later on.

The horse is a herd animal, and it is important for foals and young horses to experience a herd in order to learn herd "language."

In this book I talk about my personal approach to handling foals. If you're planning to get a foal, however, you should not go by what just one particular book says. Always use your own common sense and get help from grown-ups whom you trust and who know a lot about horses. As for me, I think it's good to have two people to train a foal. Then you can help and support each other, and that gives a feeling of security both for the two of you and for the foal.

PLANNING

The first thing to consider if you want to get a foal is the quality of the mare and the stallion. Even if you have a mare that you love dearly, it's not necessarily the best idea to breed her in order to have an offspring from your favorite horse. Sometimes it may be better to buy a foal. Then you can decide on the gender – whether you want a filly (girl) or a colt (boy), and you can shop for a foal with good qualities.

If you wish to breed a mare, it should have a nice conformation, be free of any major faults, have a good temper, and it should be able to pass on certain qualities to the foal. It's important to remember that even if you love your mare a lot, you'll never get that exact horse again, even if you get a foal from her.

With regard to the stallion, it's important to find one that suits the mare. Rule number one is, of course, to make sure you are allowed to breed with this stallion. Every country has its own rules and regulations for breeding, and you'll have to check what these are first. Let's say you have a mare that you think is good enough to breed. Maybe she has received prizes at horse shows, or has excellent riding qualities that you wish her to pass on. First you need to decide if you want to keep the foal or if you want to sell it. That goes for all breeds. If you are going to sell the foal, you should first check to see if there is a market for selling the particular breed you have, and how likely it is that you'll be able to sell the foal once it has been weaned from its mother.

It isn't always easy to sell a foal, and it costs money to feed and maintain it until you find a buyer. It takes time, money and a lot of hard work if you are going to keep it for yourself – especially if this was not your original intention. Without wanting to, you might end up having two horses instead of one.

Once the decision has been made, however, and you're starting the process of breeding, the real excitement begins. At least that's how it is at our stud farm when we're planning the breeding season. The search for the perfect stallion is on!

As mentioned earlier, it is important to find a stallion that satisfies the requirements determined by each horse breed organization. This is necessary in order to register the horse and get the proper papers for it, so it will have the right to participate in shows, and so the breed will be maintained as much as possible. Every breed organization keeps a studbook, or listing of stallions registered for breeding, and usually also a directory of stud farms. These are places where you can seek help, in addition to the Internet, in order to find out which characteristics the various stallions have.

You should always go to see the stallion for yourself, because a video or a picture doesn't necessarily show what the stallion really is like.

Then you can also evaluate the temper of the stallion, which may possibly be one of the most important factors. Information about a behavioral vice, such as cribbing and weaving, is not always disclosed. These are major flaws that I personally do not want to allow into the breed; hence I steer away from stallions with those kinds of problems.

Horse owners should inform potential buyers about such faults if they're selling a horse, but the information is not required for breeding, and it's therefore a good idea to look for it. Some breed associations won't certify horses with this type of fault for breeding.

It's a good idea to ask a breeder, judge or breed organization for advice. It's important to be honest with yourself and bring up any faults the mare might have, in order to avoid breeding with stallions that might enforce the problem. Remember that no horse is perfect. Also seek help in checking the stallion's and the mare's bloodlines, to see if they are suited to each other. Breeders are usually good at this because they have experience with a variety of combinations. That's why it is important to have a pedigree, so that you'll know exactly what is in the mare's bloodlines. A pedigree is an essential tool for a breeder. The stallion's dam line is of great importance for continued breeding, and it's important to take some time to study the bloodlines carefully. By that I mean that you should look at a few generations back – and not only at the stallion's parents.

Peleng – A very important and famous stallion in our breeding program.

NATURAL BREEDING

The most common way to breed a horse is to have the owner of the mare transport her to the stallion at stud when she's in heat. The mare will normally stay at the stud farm for a few days if it's far away, but some people prefer to take their horse home immediately afterwards. This will be okay as long as you choose a stallion that is reasonably close to where you live.

Some stud farms use breeding hobbles on the mare. These are leg restraints that prevent the mare from kicking backward and potentially injuring the stallion. Not all mares will tolerate the use of such hobbles, and personally I don't like to have a bunch of ropes and straps around the legs of the horses. However, there is a high risk of injury to the stallion if the mare kicks, so I totally understand it if the stud farm wants to take precautions.

At our stud farm the mares have their hind shoes removed, which is pretty much taken for granted in most places, but we do not use breeding hobbles. We clearly state that breeding hobbles are not used during live cover (breeding), and we also say that if the mare doesn't stand satisfactorily (that is, if her heat, or estrous cycle, isn't strong enough), she will not be covered. If the mare's heat isn't strong enough for her to stand calmly, chances are she won't get pregnant. There are also some mares that simply won't have anything to do with the stallion, and in such cases you may be better off using artificial insemination.

Another method of natural breeding is pasture breeding, where the stallion is put in the same pasture with the mares. There are some horse breeds where breeding is regularly done this way. A certain number of mares are put into a large pasture with the stallion. This is, for instance, a very common breeding method for Icelandic, Norwegian Fjord and Døle horses as well as various pony breeds. The mares are led into the pasture and stay on a lead rope until the stallion comes out. At that point all the horses are released at the same time.

This is the most natural method, and several of the mares will usually end up pregnant. The drawback of this method is that it's not always easy to make sure that all of them have been covered, nor is it easy to determine the exact time when the foal will be born.

We used a variation of this method to breed our own mares with our old stallion, Peleng. But we did it by first holding the mare and having her covered, and then allowing the mare and stallion to run in the pasture together. This worked great in the case of Peleng. We never had any major injuries with him, even though occasionally the mares made it perfectly clear that they weren't interested, and that he'd better stay away.

THE PREGNANT MARE

The mare's heat, or estrous cycle as it's also called, usually lasts from five to seven days, but this can vary a lot between mares. Some have shorter and some have longer estrous cycles. There are about 21 days between each estrous cycle, or heat. The estrous cycle is the strongest in spring and gets steadily weaker in fall and winter. The strongest estrous cycles usually occur from March until June.

It may be a good idea to plan breeding a year ahead. Think about what time would be best to have the foal. You may have to consider summer pasture and the availability of a stall. Foaling should also occur at a time when you're able to be in the stable and keep watch during the foaling.

A mare is usually pregnant for 11 months and 11 days, but plus or minus three weeks is also considered normal. Technically, that means that the foal could arrive right before the eleventh month. Even so, it's more likely that the pregnancy lasts at least eleven months, so we usually count on that. Most horses are impregnated toward the end of the mare's estrous cycle, because that's when the egg is released. We therefore estimate the birth date for our horses to be about 11 months from the last cover.

Be aware that there is no guarantee that the mare will get pregnant in the first breeding attempt. And if so, you need time for another cover before it's too late. We think May is a nice month to start breeding attempts. At that time the estrous cycle is strong and we have a few months to get the mare pregnant. If you live in a place with a warm climate, it's perfectly okay to start earlier, too. As for us, we live in a cold climate far north, which makes an early spring birth more of a problem because it's often too cold for the horses to be outside. Young foals should not be outside in chilly rain and wind for too long. Some breeds are hardier than others, but regardless, it's a good idea to keep an extra watch over little ones in the beginning.

Qatana pregnant

SUPPLEMENTS BEFORE BREEDING

Mares that are substantially overweight have a harder time getting pregnant. Your mare should be in good, normal shape before breeding. It may be easier for a thinner horse that's in the process of gaining weight to get pregnant, than for a mare that's overweight.

There are a variety of natural vitamins and minerals that will help a mare's fertility. These also protect against insect attacks and contribute to good fetal development.

Beta Carotene is an important provitamin (a substance converted into a vitamin by animal tissue) in forming the fertility hormone. This vitamin is easily broken down by stored hay and grass and it's therefore a good idea to give this supplement to the mare before breeding. It also makes her estrous cycle stronger, and after the foal is born it will boost the vitamin A content of the mare's milk. This protects the foal against infection.

Vitamin E is also important for good fertility. The required amount of Vitamin B increases during pregnancy in order to keep the uterus lining healthy and strong. Vitamin F helps the mare absorb and utilize fat-soluble vitamins. The broodmare has an increased need for these particular nutrients, and in the spring we give all the mares that will be covered a Beta Carotene supplement.

Right after they've been covered, we allow the mares to take it easy for a while. It's a good idea to avoid stress during this period. After a while, for instance while the mare is in summer pasture, it's time to start up training again. It's no problem to ride a pregnant mare, but in Norway it's not permitted to enter her in shows or competition riding between the fifth and eleventh month of pregnancy. Neither is it permitted to enter a mare whose foal is younger than six months. Foals should never be brought along to a show. I would also like to advise anyone who has a pregnant mare to use common sense when riding her. It's better to take it a little easier and not demand as much from the horse as you normally would. The mare needs to save her strength for the foal when it arrives, and the first thing a horse will do if there are problems along the way, is abandon the foal.

Do continue, however, to keep exercising the horse, to make sure it stays healthy and doesn't get totally out of shape. We usually reduce activity considerably during the last three months of pregnancy, only taking her for walking rides in the woods. The mare likes to have some activity; otherwise she could easily get bored. Some may have a reaction to the saddle, and if so, you could ride bareback.

FEEDING A PREGNANT MARE

The mare's food has a huge impact on the foal's development. During the pregnancy the fetus gets all of its nutrients through the placenta. This happens without the mare's body taking into consideration its own needs for minerals and vitamins. Therefore it's essential that the mare be fed a good diet with enough vitamins and minerals to cover both of their needs. In addition, in the winter you may want to give her Beta Carotene supplements in order to boost the foal's immune system.

During the first months of pregnancy, the mare should get the same food it usually eats. If you have a well-balanced feeding plan where the mare has access to good food with roughage and enough vitamins and minerals, that's ideal. Toward the end of the pregnancy, however, it's a good idea to add a little extra feed.

The need for protein and energy increases drastically during the last three months of pregnancy. Also the required amounts of minerals and vitamins change. You can't just increase the amount of food; you'll have to find the right kind of food intended for pregnant mares. The nutritional balance of the food is important in order to make sure the mare doesn't get too much cornstarch and protein. Pregnant mares that get too much starch could easily develop laminitis.

We use a specially formulated feed for pregnant and nursing mares. Since this feed is already adjusted to the special needs of the pregnant mare, it's easier to make sure that the horse gets the vitamins and minerals it needs at daily feedings.

FOALING

It's not always easy to tell exactly when the mare is ready to foal. We've been fooled more than once, while other times we can tell that something is definitely happening just by looking at the horse. The udder usually gets full of milk and a waxy secretion builds up on the nipples. These are signs that the moment of foaling is near. Sometimes milk may be dripping for up to a couple of days before the foal comes, though, so if you're not sure how this exact horse reacts when foaling, it may be difficult to predict the exact time. Other horses may not have the waxy secretions at all before the foal arrives. However, you can often see it in the horse's eyes that something is happening. She'll get a different look in her eyes, probably because of having contractions, which hurt. Some horses will be sweating heavily when the time is near, while others look just fine. The muscles around the pelvis get very soft and relaxed, and the vulva swells.

A newborn Shetland foal

There are specially designed alarms for mares, which are useful if several mares are due to foal at different times.

Most foals are born in the early morning hours. Nature does this to give them a better opportunity to stand and follow their mothers before night falls.

Right before foaling, the mare gets uneasy, and she may scrape the ground. Some may roll around on the ground, while others just lie down and then get back up again. At this point the foal is ready and positioned with its head and forelegs toward the birth canal. The mare lies down when she's ready to push out the foal. The contractions will push the forelegs and head out first. The water bag may rupture right away, but sometimes it can be so tough that it doesn't rupture by itself at all. If that happens, the foal will emerge enclosed by the membrane, and if it doesn't manage to move its head enough to make the bag burst, you'll have to open the bag so the foal can breathe.

The delivery itself (from the moment the mare lies down and starts pushing) usually takes 15 to 20 minutes. If the mare takes longer than that, something is probably wrong. It may be that the legs are not in the right position, though this is usually not a problem.

The newborn foal has a padding on its hooves that protects the mare from being injured. This padding quickly goes away and the hooves harden.

It's important to let the mare lie still after the foaling, allowing blood to run through the umbilical cord to the foal. The mare will usually get up after a few minutes and whinny at her foal. She licks it, which helps stimulate the foal's blood circulation. She will also be imprinted by the foal's smell and thereby accept it as her own foal.

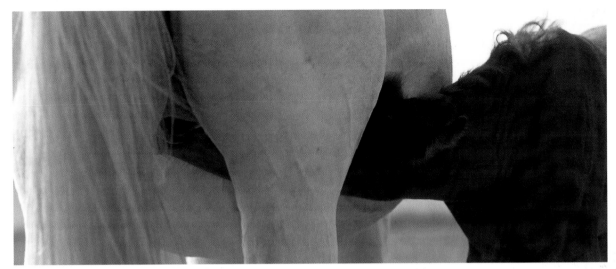
The first milk is very important for the foal.

It doesn't take very long after the foal comes out for it to try to stand. It may take anywhere from 15 to 40 minutes after it's born until it can stand up on tottering legs. The foal will still look a little squashed and tattered. After it has gotten to its legs, it'll start searching for milk. Some foals find the udder without any problem, while other foals seem to be completely helpless. It's therefore important to keep watching and make sure that the foal really drinks the milk.

That first milk is absolutely necessary for the foal. It's called colostrum, and it contains various essential proteins and antibodies that protect the foal against infections. It further contributes to allowing the intestines to start functioning correctly. Even a delay of a few hours could make the foal less resistant to infection. If the foal doesn't find the milk by itself within a couple of hours, it may be a good idea to milk the mare and give colostrum to the foal from a bottle.

At least then it will get those important antibodies, and you can take more time afterwards to help the foal find the udder.

It is always a very special moment witnessing a foal being born. You're so anxious for everything to go well, and it's equally exciting every time. The foal sometimes needs help finding the udder, but allow it as much time as possible to try to find it by itself, and don't make a lot of fuss unless it's necessary. The mare also has to expel the afterbirth (the placenta) before the birthing process is really over. Never try to pull this out by yourself, because it could be very dangerous if any leftover parts remain in the uterus afterwards. If several hours go by without the mare expelling the placenta by herself, you'll need to call the vet. The mare may get an infection if she goes too long with the remains of the pregnancy inside. There is also a higher risk of contracting laminitis with this kind of problem.

Make sure the foal has a bowel movement. The first stools are often hard and may be diccifult for the foal to get out. If that happens you could use a small tube with a mini-enema to help the foal. Once the foal has had its bowel movement and has had some milk, we make a nice, warm porridge for the mare, and after that they're left alone. It may be tempting to stay with the foal a little longer, but the mare will relax better if she gets to be alone now and have a chance to adapt to this new little miracle that has entered her life.

Make sure they have plenty of soft bedding and enough straw and shavings at the bottom of the stall, so the foal won't get hurt when it starts trying to stand up. You have to count on it falling a few times. A soft layer on the floor will also be important in the future, to keep the foal's joints from getting scraped or injured.

We don't believe in imprint training of foals immediately after they are born. Imprint training (to imprint human handling on the foal) is done in order to teach the foal to accept humans right from birth. You touch the foal and rub it with a plastic bag, to condition it not to be afraid of strange sounds. In addition, you lift its legs and tap its hooves in order to get the foal used to sounds and sensations that it will encounter when the farrier comes into the picture. (There is a lot more to imprint training than what I have mentioned here).

Imprint training is probably a fine method for some people, but for us it didn't really work. We were uncomfortable with all the hustle and bustle around a newborn foal during the first days. To us it is more important that the foal gets to be with its mother and learn the horse's language first. The humans can wait. We don't usually have any trouble teaching our foals all kinds of stuff, even if they are a little older when we start handling them.

After about three weeks, the foal starts gradually eating things other than its mother's milk, and at this point it's a good idea to give it an extra supply of energy feed especially formulated for foals. That way the foal gets all the vitamins and minerals it needs. The foal should also have a daily supplement in the summer while it's in the pasture. Although this may be troublesome to give, the foal will benefit greatly from it.

During the first half year of its life, the foal goes through a tremendous development, and it's important that it gets the right nutrition to ensure proper growth of bones and tendons. After six months some of the "growth zones," specific areas of its body that develop such tissue, muscle and bone, will close, and whatever the foal has not made use of by then, will not be able to develop later.

It's no cause for panic if your foal's legs look a little strange the first couple of weeks. A foal doesn't have much room inside the womb, and it needs a little time to straighten itself out. If you have any doubts, you can ask a vet to look at it. After a couple of weeks you should see clear improvement. If not, it's usually possible to correct the legs of small foals.

Over the course of time while the horse grows from foal to a full-grown horse, it may sometimes have swollen joints. This is often a sign of growth, in which case it's important to let the horse rest as much as possible. However, be aware that it could also be a sign of sickness if the horse has severely swollen joints and has not been hurt. It's better to call the vet too often than not often enough. Loose bone fragments are a problem with some horse breeds, and this should be looked at if your vet advises it.

Carefully monitor the health of your foal, and always contact a vet if you notice that the foal has a fever or seems fatigued. It doesn't always take much for a foal's immune system to be weakened. A foal isn't all that strong. It is extremely important to provide early treatment for a sick foal, otherwise its deveopment will fall behind in so many ways.

Vaccinations against equine flu and tetanus should be given when the foal is about six months old. The foal's initial vaccination includes immunization against both diseases, with a booster dose given a few weeks later. A third dose against equine flu is given within six months, and then a flu and tetanus booster.

If you intend to enter the horse in eventings or shows, it should have regular vaccinations at least once a year. Your vet will recommend a timetable for the equine flu vaccination, as well as rhinopneomonitis, equine encephalomyelitis and tetanus. Also, depending on where you live, the vet will also vaccinate against rabies, strangles and Potomac horse fever. Some horses may have a reaction to the vaccines, but fortunately this doesn't happen very often.

Make sure you don't overfeed your foal or young horse. A young horse should never be fat; it could lead to bone and skeleton damage.

Remember that your horse's teeth need to be looked after. We usually check the bit to see if the teeth hit it in a way that allows them to chew properly. When the horse is a year old, either before or after summer pasture, we have the vet check the teeth and file them if needed, to make sure they'll be okay. This should be done at least once a year, and it's especially important before you put a bit in the horse's mouth. Some horses may grow what we call wolf teeth. These will usually interfere with the bit and should be removed.

When you first start training a young horse, it's important to use tendon support boots or bandages. This is particularly important if you're doing lunging or loose jumping. Use this kind of protection to avoid leg injuries. It is also important when you first shoe the horse. I have to admit that we haven't always adhered to this rule ourselves, as may be seen by the pictures in this book. However, the most important thing is to take them off immediately after the training session.

Lunging, or exercising a horse (usually in a circle) on the end of a long rope, is typical early training for young horses before they learn to accept a bit and saddle. Long lining (also called double lunging, with two lines attached) is a great European technique for ground training young horses, although not typically used in the Americas. For my own part, I don't really like long lining on the lunge – that is, in a circle as if you're lunging. It gets to be pretty hard on your legs. Furthermore, it's difficult to keep a light touch on the rein, unless you're exceptionally good at it.

On the other hand, long lining your horse while you walk behind it and let it get used to having reins and straps hanging loose on the side, is great training. If you have the opportunity to take your young horse along as an in-hand horse, that is also a very good way to train it.

Pedigree	SR EL Patron	Peleng SU	Nabeg SU	Arax PL
				Nomenklatura SU
			Palmira SU	Salon SU
				Ptashka SU
		Qatana DK	El Shaklan DE	Shaker El Masri EG
				Estopa ES
			Qatar DE	Kiew ES
				Huca ES

RINE ARABIAN STUD

Our Arabian stud farm is located on the west coast of Norway, in a place called Kvernland, south of the city of Stavanger (where the International PONY offices are located). We have been breeding Arabian horses since 1994. Rine, who co-owns the farm with her husband, also rents stable space to other horse owners, and we have a total of 45 horses in the stable. I met Rine 14 years ago through another friend who was also working with Arabian horses. After a while Rine and I started working together, and we agreed to start breeding Russian Arabian horses. We searched a long time for a big, fine-looking mare with a wonderful temper.

We found our dream horse, Asmena, at Countess Penelope Lewenhaupt's stable in Sweden. Asmena became the foundation of our stud farm and represented everything we wanted to breed in the future. To us the most important factor has always been the horse's temper. Next comes movement and ridability. Arabian horses should, of course, also be beautiful. Asmena originally came from Germany, and when we got her she was pregnant by an Egyptian stallion named Shahin.

Another mare we acquired through the Countess in Sweden was Primanka, born at a Russian State Stud named Tersk, and already 18 years old when she came. Pinczow was our first stud stallion. He was two years old when we found and bought him at an auction in Holland. He was, and still is, a very valuable stud stallion to us. He gives us type, size, movement and temper that are suitable for riding. His foals are usually the ones that sell first.

Next we bought Qatana, the only "El Shaklan" mare in Norway. This beautiful, sparkling white mare was simply a dream as a broodmare, riding horse, and as a creature. She was the gentlest thing you ever saw, and never did anything wrong during the time we had her. If somebody didn't know how to ride at all, we could always put them on top of Qatana. She would make sure that nothing bad happened. When kids were riding her, she always walked so carefully and calmly, it looked as if she was deliberately trying to help us keep them in the saddle.

Qatana had Spanish Egyptian lines and her sire was world-famous for his great offspring.

The last stud stallion we acquired was Peleng. He was Russian and had lived a life among the big horses. He had many great offspring, both in the US and in Europe, but as he got older he lived a peaceful and quiet life together with his mares here at our farm.

A FOAL FROM PELENG

We had always wanted to have Qatana covered (bred) by some exciting stallion abroad, but every year something got in the way of our plans. In the end we had her covered by Pinczow. The foals she had with him were great-looking horses with big movements and beautiful tempers. When we got Peleng it didn't take us long to decide to use him for breeding. In the spring of 2000 Qatana was covered by Peleng.

On the foggy morning of May 13, 2001, Rine called and asked me to come over because Qatana had had her foal. She was outside in the field, and early in the dawn she had given birth to a beautiful colt foal. Rine hadn't been aware of the birth until the foal was out. It wasn't the first time Qatana fooled us and had her foal all by herself. She was an old mare who knew what she was doing, but we still preferred to be there, just in case something happened.

By the time we got there, Qatana had already gotten rid of the afterbirth and was taking care of things by herself. The foal was nursing, so there was nothing for us to do, except admire the beautiful little colt (boy horse). Of course, he looked a little scruffy at first. The fog was also making things damp, which didn't help his looks any. Foals are always a little frail and funny looking at first, but after a few days they start looking much better and taking on a more "normal" shape. The legs of the newborn colt foal were just fine, with no unevenness. We were glad about that. I guess we had actually been hoping for a filly (girl horse), but as long as the mare and the foal were both okay, we were just happy everything went well.

It's always a relief when the actual foaling is over. Even though it usually goes well, there are certain risks that are always at the back of our minds, and of course we can't help worrying about things that could potentially happen.

Qatana was the perfect mother. She always raised her foals in a nice way, corrected their faults, and she had plenty of milk. The problem was that she herself totally fell apart. While her foals were bursting with health, she would get thinner and thinner, and there was nothing we could do about it. Even though we fed her well, it seemed hopeless. If she didn't have a foal at foot, there was a chance of fattening her up over the winter, but this time she got alarmingly thin after she had her foal. Still, she seemed fit and ran proudly around in the field showing him off to us.

We had decided that if we ever had a colt by Qatana and Peleng we would keep him at the stud, at least for a few years. Qatana didn't have the same dam line as our other broodmares, and this stallion could therefore be an exciting addition to Pinczow, our youngest breeding stallion.

Deciding on a new foal's name is always a big deal. It is not an easy task either, because we want to make sure the name suits the horse well. This time the little colt was named SR El Patron. SR is for the stud, "Stutteri Rine" as it is called in Norwegian. We always put SR in front of the name of our offspring. El Patron is a Spanish nobleman, and we thought that was a fitting name for this handsome little stallion, which had Spanish blood in his dam line, from his mother's mother, Qatar, and his mother's father, El Shaklan.

Qatana and Peleng

THE FIRST FEW WEEKS

We put Qatana and her foal in a paddock with our old mare, Asmena, the first few weeks after foaling. Asmena was not pregnant, but she and Qatana had always been together, and were very comfortable with each other. The other mares were kept in a different field. They had given birth to their foals earlier, and we had several foals from Peleng that year. When it came time to let the other mares out in the summer pasture, we kept Qatana in the field right by the stable. We wanted to look after her more closely and were feeding her supplemental feeds. That helped, and after a while we could let her go with the other mares, so she could enjoy the summer pasture too.

The pasture is big, about 30 acres, and contains all of our mares. In addition, Rine takes in a few more mares for the season. The mares' pasture is a little hilly. It

Qatana and her newborn foal

borders on the woods, and a lake where the horses drink, and when it gets really warm a few of them may even wade into the water, splashing water with their forelegs in order to cool off. There are no trees inside the pasture, but trees have been planted around the perimeter as a windbreak. The horses can always find a place where the wind doesn't blow too much. When it gets hot they'll stand at the top of the pasture where there's always a little breeze and the least amount of flies. The climate in Norway is generally extreme, but it is milder here, with some snow in the winter and quite a bit of rain. The pasture season is usually from May to September, making it nice to have the foals born between March and May.

Ωgo out in the pasture. Petting and cuddling the foals is important in the beginning. Later we put a halter on and lead them out next to their mothers. We lift the legs a little and tap the underside of their hooves with our hands. Afterwards we groom them all over, including the legs. It is also important to stroke the foal on the face and over the ears, getting it used to being touched on the head. How much we do of this kind of training varies a little, depending on the foal. Some of them couldn't care less what you do to them, while others are more skeptical about being touched. When it's time for summer pasture, both the foals and adult horses are given time off from training. During this time we only do worming, and check that everything is okay. The mares are given worm medicine before they go out in the pasture, and the foals are wormed if they show signs of loose stool and every six weeks after that, for as long as they are in the pasture.

Worming practices vary in different countries. In some countries you can't buy worm medicine unless the stool has shown signs of worm first.

SR El Patron

I believe in raising foals as naturally as possible, in a herd. For this reason we try to provide a separate pasture for only mares with foals and young horses. Our experience is that if we try to mix in too many geldings there will be trouble, and it doesn't take much to harm a foal. I have personally witnessed a gelding attack a newborn foal, and it was one of the ugliest things I've ever seen. The gelding practically turned into a predator, grabbing the foal by the neck with his mouth and thrashing it around. All I could do was scream and holler, while throwing big rocks at the attacker in sheer desperation. Fortunately the foal recovered. They have an amazing resiliency, but since then not a single gelding has ever again been allowed into the same pasture as the foals.

During the first months the foals pretty much stay close to their mothers, but gradually they get a little braver and start wandering off by themselves around the pasture, while the mothers usually watch them from a distance. Colt foals will start playing with each other as they grow a little bigger. Filly foals join in the games sometimes, but generally the colt foals are more active. They like being around other foals their own size and will often sleep near each other – sometimes almost on top of each other.

El Patron really enjoyed playing with the other foals. He had a special friend named SR Nova. Nova means new star. These two were the only colt foals in the herd, and they quickly bonded with each other. El Patron and Nova's days were all about playing, sleeping and maybe teasing their mothers a little. Qatana was a patient mom, but sometimes, if El Patron crossed the line, she would very quickly put him in his place with a little nip and a scolding look. He learned fast how to behave and paid attention to the little lessons his mom gave him.

El Patron on his thin long legs

El Patron playing around

Early in the morning and in the evening the foals tend to be livelier, and then the rest of the herd tend to perk up as well. They might all join in a lively gallop, going a few rounds around the field. El Patron used to think it was a lot of fun to try to get the sheep to join in. He would look at them, rear up, run a little and then stop to see if they would follow. Sometimes he'd get some young sheep or a lamb to run along for a few yards at least. When they did, he was delighted, continuing to rear up and run sideways while looking at them. Unfortunately the sheep didn't usually care about his games for very long, so El Patron was left to gallop a few rounds alone to get rid of his energy.

Before the fall weather is upon us, we move the mares back to the fields by the stable, in order to watch them more closely. By then they've been covered again, and it's just a good idea to keep them around the stallion in case they're still in heat and may not have gotten pregnant yet.

FALL

In September food starts getting scarce, and at that point the horses have to come inside at night. We feed them morning and evening, in addition to letting them graze outside. El Patron and a filly foal named SR Naomi were born in May, a few months later than the other foals. All together we had six foals from Peleng that year. The four who were born in February and March were separated from their mothers when we took them inside in the fall. El Patron and Naomi got to stay in their childhood paradise for a few more months. The four who where separated from their mothers were placed in their own stalls in pairs. The mothers were given an extra week in the pasture without supplemental feeding. (That's a good way to reduce milk production, by not giving the mares any supplemental feed, and only letting them graze on grass with less nutrition.) We always watch the mares closely at this point, to make sure they don't develop udder infections. It is sometimes a good idea to squeeze out some of the excess milk for a few days. Not all mares will tolerate being separated from their foals in this way. Some of them have to be weaned in a more gradual way to keep them from going crazy and running around, neighing hysterically. In such cases we place the foal in a stall next to its mother at night, and let them be together outside during the day. Maybe this sounds like a more sympathetic way to do it, but for some mares it actually works better the other way.

As far as we are concerned, we like it better when we can separate the mares and foals cold turkey. That way life in the stable gets peaceful again a little faster, both for the mares and the foals. Once the little ones are on their own we put them in a separate section of the stable. Our stable is divided into several small sections, hence we have a separate "nursery" for the foals. This is a small corner where the stalls are not as big as the rest. The ceiling is not as high, so it wouldn't work to have regular stalls there anyway. In this corner the foals are also further away from their mothers. And because they can't see them the whole time, it results in less neighing and noise inside the stable. Since we put two foals together at a time, we try to figure out which ones have become best friends. However, we switch them around after a while, to avoid having them get too attached to one particular horse.

It's usually best to keep stallions with stallions and mares with mares, but if that is not possible, at least try not to combine two horses who are at opposite ends of the social hierarchy, or pecking order (for instance a dominant horse with a non-aggressive horse). If you don't you'll have problems with the horses fighting over food.

You may want to keep the foals inside during the first few days. If you let a foal outside on the first day after

El Patron is growing.

El Patron is looking for his mom.

it has been separated from its mother, it will most likely try to run through the fence when it hears her call. That means an increased risk of injury. If you decide to bring the foal outside, make sure you take it on a lead rope to a place where it cannot see or hear its mother.

Older mares are usually not a problem when you bring them outside. They know what's happening, and even though they run along the fence calling for their foals at first, they'll soon settle down. With young mares that haven't had a foal before, we wait a while before we let them out. The horse could easily get injured if it runs through the fence in order to get to the foal. And it doesn't take too many days before even a young mare will settle down.

The foals are usually brought outside after four or five days. At first they get to be in a smaller area right behind the stable. They're safe there, and they won't be right next to the mares. Actually, they can't even see the mares from this paddock.

Now is the time for them to start learning a few things. The foals will be a little confused at first, being without their mothers, but after they've been outside together for a while and start getting used to the new situation, it's time to continue their training.

This is also a great opportunity for a human to bond with the foal. At this point the foal doesn't have a mother to consider anymore. From now on, the humans are its caretakers and will become its most important contacts, besides the other foal that it may be sharing a stall with.

El Patron was separated from Qatana the quick way. She went directly back to the pasture while El Patron got a new filly friend, Naomi. They got along just fine. It doesn't always work to put a filly foal with a colt, but El Patron behaved like a gentleman. He didn't act very bossy or pushy, the way colt foals tend to. They shared a feed tray and didn't even fight over the food. After a few days, we put them with the other foals outside, and they continued to stay together, even though El Patron had been playing with Nova all summer.

As for us, we kept busy taking the foals for walks on a lead rope, lifting their legs, grooming them, and caring for them. A lot of children come to our stable, and they are allowed to visit with the foals, as well as cuddle and brush them. Taking them for walks, however, has to be done by a grown-up in the beginning. The same applies to the jobs of lifting their legs and putting halters on, until the foals get more used to these things.

The foal doesn't need to walk very far the first few times, because it may find it a little frightening to be out on it own. It isn't always easy to get the foal to go where you want it to, either. Don't expect too much in the first few days. Try to make the walks a positive experience, and give the foal a lot of praise when it goes where you want it to. Try also to place a limit on treats. It's better to stroke the foal on the neck and to reward it with praise. While you're out walking the foal, you can practice getting it to stand still as well.

The following may be the most important things to teach a foal:

1. To walk nicely on a lead rope.

2. To stand still when you tell it to.

It's okay to teach the foal to stop on a certain command – either by using your voice or, for instance, by lifting your hand. Foals learn easily, and it won't take very many attempts before they have learned to stop. It may be harder to teach them to stand still. Be patient with this. It doesn't do any good to get angry with a foal, because it simply doesn't understand what you want it to do. Don't try to train your foal on a day when you're in a bad mood. On those days it's better to just cuddle it, and leave it at that. It's important to make all learning a positive experience for the foal, and to do the training when you feel up to it.

At the beginning we tied El Patron inside his stall while we brushed and groomed him. We always use a quick-release knot or panic snap, so that if the horse gets scared and pulls he can be freed quickly. Panic, however, wasn't exactly the first word that came to mind with El Patron. He was such a calm and sensible young colt, and didn't show any reaction at all to being tied up. Some foals will start pulling and will try to sit down; if this happens the key is to remain calm. By remaining calm you'll help the foal collect itself and start thinking. Get the foal to take a step forward so it won't feel the resistance in the halter anymore.

Make sure you don't take too long. It's better to spend only a few minutes on this in the beginning. If you tie the foal and expect it to stay tied up for a long time, it will usually result in the foal getting scared, and then it will start tugging and pulling on the rope. This could lead to problems later on.

As soon as El Patron was comfortable being tied up in the stall, we moved out to the stable hallway. Out there he was a little unsure the first time, but he remained calm, and seemed to figure out that it wasn't any worse being tied up by a chain than by a rope. We didn't keep him tied up very long in the beginning, and he was given a treat afterwards, to make sure he had a positive association with it.

The first time we wanted him to walk alone out the stable door, El Patron just looked at us with big, huge eyes. He seemed totally shocked. Going out the door all by himself – with no other horses walking along? Forget it! It's no use trying to pull on a foal's halter if the foal is dead set against going. But since there are always two of us working together with the foals, it helped that one of us could give him a slap on the behind. Then he really took off, jumping through the doorway as if there was a big hurdle in the way. Hmmm... maybe we had a talented jumper on our hands...

Once through those first steps of his education, El Patron was ready for his next lesson. The next step was learning to be washed. Horses should be trained to get a bath. We didn't use soap the first few times, but started with gentle and careful rinsing of the legs. To some horses it can be pretty scary to go into the wash stall, hence it may be a good idea to practice this too at first. El Patron didn't care much for having water on his legs the first time, but he accepted it, and the next day things went much smoother. We are careful not to try to do too much all at once, but just give the horse one small but good lesson that it can build on later. And it is very easy to scare a horse at this stage. If something goes wrong, you'll have to work very hard to reestablish trust.

Get somebody to help you by holding the horse, or have them hose it off while you hold the horse. The following applies whenever you do anything that has to do with training a horse: Hurry slowly, and have fun in the process. It is a lot of fun to work with young horses. They are all about fun and games, and they are incredibly eager to learn. If you succeed in keeping the horse interested and try not to do too much at once, you'll have a horse that likes to work with you. Be aware that foals and young horses don't have a very long attention span. Don't force things. Just practice something for a few minutes, and then allow the lesson to sink in. It's better to do something else before you try it again.

Remember also that a foal should be allowed to be a foal, and to play and have fun with other horses its own age.

It's important to reward every little accomplishment the foal makes along the way. Use your voice and stroke the horse on the neck while you tell it how good it is. Treats should be saved for big occasions, for example

Learning to be washed.

when the horse has done something really well, or when you've been practicing something very difficult. The horse understands praise very well, and the more you praise it, the faster it will learn. If you use too many treats, especially with colt foals, you may quickly get a horse that's rude and nips at people in order to get something. It's better to put a little extra food in their tray after the lesson. Then you don't have to give so much from your hand.

FARRIER: Preparing the foal for the farrier, or blacksmith (the person who shoes horses) is important. That's why it's a good idea to get the foal used to having its legs lifted right from the start, and to be tapped under the hooves with a brush or a hammer. Some foals need to have their hooves corrected when they're quite small, while others are fine until they are separated from their mother. Regardless, when the farrier is coming for the first time it's important to prepare the foal so it doesn't get scared. That can easily happen if the foal is not at all used to having its legs touched. And that's the owner's responsibility, not the farrier's. Of course, some foals will still have a reaction when a stranger is lifting and pulling on their legs. We just have to accept that people do things in different ways, and the farrier's ways may be very different from the way you do it. Therefore you should be particular about using a farrier who's patient and takes his or her time, so the foal's first experience with this will be a positive one. Make sure to tell the farrier beforehand that the horse is a foal, and ask them to schedule a little extra time for the job in order to avoid a negative experience. You should also get everything ready in the stable before the farrier arrives, preparing a safe place where the foal will stand. Make sure it has peace and quiet. It would be very frustrating both for the foal and the farrier to deal with the hustle and bustle of other horses going in and out, or squeaky wheelbarrows going by.

El Patron and the other foals began to go outside together without the adult horses. For one thing, we thought they needed a little time to feel confident with themselves and the other horses in the herd. Some adult horses tend to chase the little ones away. If so, it's good to let them have a chance to develop trust in their friends, and to learn where the borders of the paddock or the field are. It's easy for an innocent little foal to lose its head if a big, aggressive horse starts chasing it. It may forget to pay attention to where it's going.

Even though our horses are Arabians and the weather is sometimes pretty poor around here in the fall, we don't use covers on the foals. That's because we're worried that other foals could get caught in the straps or the covers when they play together. This is

particularly true for the colts, which are usually more active than the fillies. It's better to take them inside if the weather is truly bad. Most horses, though, can tolerate normal weather conditions. It's just that where we live, on the west coast of Norway, we have a lot of chilly wind and rain in the fall, winter and spring. The combination of wind and rain is not good for Arabian foals. We have to take this into consideration, otherwise the foals will be miserable and find no joy in being outside. If the weather is dry and cold, there is nothing to worry about. They can always run around a little to keep warm.

Cold-blooded horse breeds have totally different layers of skin and coats that are much thicker than those of Arabians. Such foals can tolerate the Norwegian west coast climate much better.
It's important that foals, regardless of breed, have a chance to develop as naturally as possible so they can grow the coats they need to get through the winter.

El Patron in the paddock with the other yearlings.

TRAILER TRAINING

It's important that foals be familiar with the trailer before you take them out for their first ride. Don't hesitate to call in professional help for the tasks that you're not very comfortable with yourself. We were very lucky to get the help of an expert on natural horsemanship. Natural horsemanship is the art of training and riding horses in a way that works with the horse's behavior, instincts and personality in an easy and kind manner, and is associated with a number of world-renowned trainers. Well, our expert happened to be very good at loading horses. To us this was a great way to teach the foals to be comfortable with the trailer. It felt good to have someone there who really knew the right body language to use, and who wouldn't do something wrong and scare the foals when they were first loaded.

Of course, we were there too, watching. We all have something to learn, because one thing is for sure – we'll never be fully trained at everything.

At this point we've been working on our own body language and can communicate our wishes to the horses easily, so we should be able to do the loading by ourselves from now on. Usually we don't have any trouble because the foals already trust us so much from our daily handling of them, that it may not occur to them to be scared when going into the trailer. But it's extremely important to know your own limitations and to not take unnecessary risks. When we train the horses for trailer loading, we do not force them. The foals are rewarded with praise for even trying to approach the trailer. We take our time and make sure everything is peaceful and quiet around the trailer. There shouldn't be a lot of traffic noise, whether it's cars or people, and no loose dogs that could potentially scare the foal. What's important is that the foal feels safe and stays calm, though of course you don't let it take the lead. You need to be a firm leader, but friendly, and not rushed. It's no catastrophe if you don't succeed in getting the foal to enter the trailer the first time, but it's definitely an advantage if you do. Do not tie up the foal inside the trailer, but take it back out right away. Personally I don't think it hurts to reward the foal with a little treat when it gets into the trailer.

Trailer training.

THE YEARLING

All foals are considered yearlings after January 1, even if they were born later in the year. Since a horses' age is determined in this way, a lot of stud farms prefer to have the foals born early in the year.

If the horse is going to be used for competition riding, shows, or regular riding, it's an advantage if it's as developed as possible when it starts competing in the events for its particular breed. Four to five months' age difference between one young horse and another could make a big difference in how much the horse has developed.

El Patron and the other yearlings at our farm got to live the good life, even after they were no longer foals. The Arabian horse is a breed that develops slowly, and we don't start training them with reins and bits when they are very young. It's fine, however, for the young horses to participate in other kinds of activities. With El Patron, we decided to sign him up for a show in the summer when he was a yearling. Provided of course that he was in reasonably good shape. Foals and yearlings have a tendency to look a little funny during the stage when they're growing a lot. We actually had several yearlings that could have been shown. Nova was pretty good looking too. With his red coat and light colored mane and tail, he pretty much looked like a fairytale horse. We also had the filly foals SR Anastacia and SR Prostsjanie. Prosti, as we called her, had lost her mother when she was only three weeks old, and we didn't think she was ready for showing. Anastacia functioned as her substitute mother, which left her out of the picture. SR Gaia and SR Naomi had both been sold during the winter. Therefore, if we were to go, it would be up to the two young colts. At this point we decided on El Patron. He was growing very nicely and evenly and didn't look as crooked as some

Training in the round pen.

of the other yearlings. In fact we might have wished that he had looked a little more "gangly," because when a horse grows as nicely and evenly as El Patron, it is often a sign that it won't grow very big.

We started with some light training right after Christmas. We took El Patron for walks in the woods, sometimes alone, and other times with Nova. In the woods there are challenges such as getting around fallen trees, tufts of grass and rocks. El Patron's idea of what was scary didn't always match our own idea of scary. He and the other horses seemed to think that big rocks along the trail were extremely dangerous. Even though the rocks were lying still and never moved, it was very spooky to pass them. This may seem illogical to us, but for the horse that is a potential prey for another animal, watching out for big rocks is a natural instinct. After all, there could be a predator hiding behind the rock – like a wolf, or maybe a hungry bear.

El Patron really enjoyed training loose in the paddock or the round pen. Then we could run after him and he could run after us. There were opportunities to sprint fast, as well as trotting in nice circles. What was most important to us, was that El Patron was having fun and was comfortable with what we were doing, and therefore we didn't put too much pressure on him. By now our young colt had become a very laid-back horse, who was not very focused on training or exercise. As a result we got a pretty good workout running after him the whole time to make him move. Sometimes it was easier to have another horse along so the two could run together. Nova was our first choice on these occasions, and the two of them had a few rounds in our indoor arena during the spring months. In the round pen, however, we would work with only one horse at a time. That way you can also practice horsemanship. People

may sometimes think we are a little crazy, the way we run after our horses, waving plastic bags in the air and shaking a can of pebbles. Our young horses, however, think this is a lot of fun and love this game. It allows them to run toward us and join in the game. We have to make sure it doesn't get to be too intense, because the horses should never be scared. This activity is supposed to be fun for them. One good sign is if the horse's tail is flying like a banner in the air and it's bending its neck and looking at you while it trots around and snorts.

Horses grow in spurts, and it's important to let them have some time off when they're in one of their big growing periods. The forelegs may look a little "open" at the knees. If that's the case, the horse may get stiff and be somewhat unwilling to run. Very often a yearling who's going through a growth spurt will lie inside its stall sleeping, simply because it is worn out. Don't try to rush a horse that's growing a lot, but allow it to relax and take it easy. You can make up for it soon enough when the horse is no longer experiencing a growth spurt. You should never put a yearling on a lunge rope; it's way too hard on its legs.

Unfortunately, when you have several horses in one stable, there are some bad things that can happen. At one point we allowed a farm in eastern Norway to borrow Bimbo, a sweet little Shetland pony. After she came back we put her outside with the other horses. We noticed an ugly sore on her nose, but assumed it was a wound from the halter having rubbed her. Well, it was not. After a couple of days we discovered that several of our Shetland ponies now had gotten strange, round marks on their heads. We were pretty desperate, because it dawned on us that this was something entirely different. We called the vet, and it was what we feared – ringworm.

Wow, what an ordeal! We called a friend in France who sent some bottles of a substance we used to wash the horses . There was a lot of scrubbing and washing, and all training had to be put on hold. This happened in February when it was cold, but all the horses had to be bathed with this stinky substance. The young horses got to learn all about showering and bathing pretty quickly that year. In addition to bathing all the horses, we had to spray the entire stable with disinfectant. Saddles, brushes, saddle blankets and everything else that had been in contact with the horses, had to be cleaned. We didn't touch the horses more than was absolutely necessary during this process, so there wasn't much cuddling going on. Out of all of our horses, only four didn't show any signs of ringworm; Gagat, an Arabian who was boarded with us, Pinczow, Peleng and Asmena. Everyone else got a touch of it. I know for sure that Gagat had ringworm when he was in Denmark, and I've been told that horses are immune to it once they've had an outbreak.

We were pretty depressed about this outbreak. One of our horses had been sold to someone in Eastern Norway, but we had to keep her with us for more than a month until the outbreak was over, before letting her go to her new home. Ringworm is extremely contagious, but it is not dangerous to a healthy horse.

It seems to me that bad things come in pairs. One morning when Rine came into the stable to feed the horses she discovered that the door to El Patron's stall was open. Everything was quiet. Where was El Patron? Then she saw Kronå, one of our trotting horses. It was standing a little further back in the stable, in the "nursery," pushed toward the wall of her stall. Rine peeked inside, and there was El Patron, in the stall with Kronå. He was lying on his back, completely still, looking at her. His legs were stuck between the tray and an iron bar, and the whole situation looked pretty serious. Rine proceeded to get Kronå out of there as El Patron started struggling and kicking, trying to turn around while his hind legs were still stuck. Rine tried to stay calm, but your heart tends to do its own thing when you get into situations like these. The important thing is to not panic, because nothing good can come of that.

Luckily El Patron managed to get out of the pinch and free himself from the iron bar. He scrambled about and eventually got to his feet on shaky legs. Nothing seemed to be broken, but there were minor cuts and bruises here and there, and he was pretty beat up. Our first concern was whether he might have injuries that we couldn't see. He stumbled back to his own stall. When I went back to Kronå's stall and looked at the place where he had been lying, I couldn't fathom how it was possible for him to have gotten in there. The horse must have crawled into that stall. There's a clearing of about three feet between the ceiling and the feed tray, and at least three feet up from the floor. That stall is so small that a horse can't even turn around in there. If he had gone in head first, he would have had to back up to get out again. To this day we have no idea how he managed it!

As I said, it is both exciting and challenging to work with horses. You never know what will happen, and that's about all you know for sure!

We were done with the ringworm ordeal, and then El Patron pulled that strange magic act, which got us all worried about him. His legs were swollen, and he got very stiff and sore, but fortunately the swelling went away after a few days. A regular training schedule hadn't been started for him yet after the ringworm outbreak, so it wasn't too inconvenient to start by leading El Patron on walks to help him loosen the stiff muscles and sore legs. I can just imagine how beat up he must have felt, though. He seemed to feel very sorry for himself, judging by his sad eyes. And I'm sure he regretted his spontaneous date with the trotter filly. Maybe he was thinking afterward, "Wow! Girls sure are dangerous things – I'd better stay away from them!"

The stiffness seemed to be gone after a few weeks, so at that point we could start a more systematic training regimen before the international horse show in Oslo, the capitol city of Norway. We really wanted to take him there, but didn't know if we could rely on him, especially if he thought up any more shenanigans.

Our round pen is about 18 yards in diameter, so the horses have a lot of room to run. There is a solid fence around it, making it safe to let young horses inside. They aren't going to try to jump over that fence in order to join the other horses. The ground cover in the pen is soft, so we can't work them too long, due to the risk of strain injury.

We didn't let El Patron run for long stretches, especially in the beginning. The round pen was, however, a perfect place for his cardio workout (exercises to raise his heart rate) as well as muscle building, without going overboard. In the beginning we used the round pen to train a couple of times a week. As time went by and we got closer to the show, we increased the training. At that point we didn't take as many walks in the woods, but spent more days practicing in the round pen. We started with 10 minutes and gradually increased it to 20 minutes. We didn't practice that long every single day, but 20

minutes was the maximum amount of time we'd train. We wanted to make sure it was still fun for the horses.

In addition to the regular training, we also had to practice using the horse trailer. The horses would be going on a long trip, about 310 miles of winding roads. We definitely wanted them to have some familiarity with traveling. El Patron had no objections to entering the horse trailer – he walked straight inside as if he had done it his whole life. Then we went for a short drive with him. He was a little uneasy at first, but he calmed down and we drove home.

El Patron is a very harmonious "guy" who doesn't really care too much about what's happening around him. He has an easygoing disposition, which makes working with him easy for us. Some horses need more time than others to figure things out, and then you just have to give them the time they need.

There's a lot of work to be done before a show; for instance, washing the horse. Their coats have to look great, of course. We hadn't managed to get El Patron's coat short enough, so we had to use hair clippers. Talk about a fuss! El Patron didn't like the clipping machine at all. We even gave him a little bit of a drug to calm him down the first time he was to be clipped, but he was still uneasy. We had to forget about his ears. We couldn't get anywhere near them, so he probably would have looked a lot more elegant than he did when we were finally done.

You're actually not allowed to give haircuts to horses of certain breeds in certain countries, so you'll have to be careful about this and check the rules first.

El Patron is ready for his first show.

THE FIRST SHOW

That spring, right after the death of our beautiful stallion Peleng following a long illness, we went to the Netherlands and France to look at Arabian horses. You know how it is, when you're looking at horses, you also talk a lot about them, and of course that brought up the topic of Peleng frequently. As a result, it was a trip with a lot of sadness, and quite a few tears were shed on the way.

But our mood lightened upon visiting a grand Arabian horse show called Tulip Cup of Deurne in the Netherlands. It is an international show that is ideal for people who want to see great horses from all over Europe. The highlight of the show was Princess Alia of Jordan's white stallion, Hillayial Ramadan. When he sailed into the arena, making a grand entrance with his tail high in the air, there wasn't a single dry eye in sight. It was a wonderful and very touching moment.

The trip to Holland gave us new inspiration to restart our training, and we set up a program for El Patron.

The show was rapidly approaching. El Patron had another round with the clipping machine, and everything went well until we got to his ears. It appeared that this was just not going to happen, so we let it go. We didn't like the idea of drugging him or using force, so we decided to make the best of things as they were. El Patron had been trained to the best of our abilities, and now he was also cleaned and groomed in every way in order to make him as beautiful as possible.

The day of our departure for the show was sunny and pleasantly warm, a great day for driving.

Loading the horses went smoothly, and we managed to stack everything we needed, food and equipment, into the trailer. You need a lot of room for everything you have to take on a trip like this, but we had plenty of room in our car this time, so we didn't have any problems.

We left home in the morning and arrived at Hellerudsletta, 19 miles north of Oslo, where the show was taking place, about nine hours later. El Patron traveled in the trailer with Armani, who was a year older, and they got along just fine. Armani had been to a show when he was a yearling, so he was experienced and knew what to expect. El Patron was much safer traveling with a horse who had done it before.

The horses had a long journey; the road between Stavanger and Oslo is pretty winding so it's not the most comfortable ride. Armani and El Patron behaved in an exemplary fashion the whole way, but were tired and worn out when they arrived. Unfortunately the floor in the show stable was kind of slippery, and several of the horses had problems and fell on it. Our horses didn't wear shoes, so it wasn't quite as bad for them. Before we put them in the stable, we led them around the show area. Afterwards we gave them food and water and let them settle down for the night. Once the horses were taken care of, it was time for us humans to relax as well. After all, we would be getting up early the next day.

When we woke up the next morning, Saturday, the weather was not promising. Heavy clouds covered the area, and as we got closer to the time for our class, it

looked as if it was going to rain. As if that wasn't bad enough, we had not yet seen the Swedish handler who was supposed to show our horse. Where was she? She hadn't arrived yet! While we waited we washed yellow spots off of our horse and brushed him until he sparkled. We used a little "shoe shine" to make him look extra shiny and pretty. We also applied a special heavy cream around his eyes and muzzle to makes his face look more striking.

Our handler, who was supposed to show our horse in the ring, simply didn't show up, and panic started growing in our camp. We couldn't reach her by phone, either. In the end, I started running around like crazy, trying to find some sneakers, because one thing was certain: we were going into the ring. Finally I borrowed some old aerobic shoes that were too small, but they would have to do. So there I was, really nervous, in uncomfortable shoes.

The first part of the program was no problem. We ran into the ring along with the yearlings. After a round of trotting and a couple of rounds of walking, the judges had seen all the stallions and we left the ring. Only the first in the class remained. The next step was worse. This time the horses went into the ring, took position in front of the judges, and were then shown at a walk as well as a trot around the ring. The ring isn't terribly big, but certainly big enough when you're like me and not trained to run much. It didn't help that the ring was slightly hilly. Downhill was fine, but turning back toward the judges we had to climb slightly uphill. My legs felt like lead after a while, and we weren't moving very fast. The point is to show the horses in a big, good-looking trot. If you can get them to put on a show with their tail in the air, it's even better.

I freely admit, there wasn't much "showing off" on our part, but we did manage to show some trotting, even if I was huffing and puffing. It was a good thing I wasn't the one being judged! Finally, we were done, and the next horse took over. Then came the never-ending minutes of waiting for scores, and after that we just had to wait until the whole class was done in order to find out the results. El Patron did reasonably well as far as scores go. He got a gold medal, which we were very happy with. And he came in fifth in class, which wasn't too bad either. He was clearly tired from the long trip across the country, so we couldn't really expect any more of him.

We spent the rest of the day looking at the other young horses, and on Sunday we headed back home after the show. Armani and El Patron behaved perfectly and walked into the trailer without any fuss or nonsense, so I guess they didn't mind going home. It was nice to see that they felt so secure and didn't hesitate entering the trailer. We saw plenty of other horses making big fusses attempting to avoid their trailers. It isn't much fun for the horse or the owner when you have to fight so hard to convince the horse that the trailer isn't dangerous.

After the horses are loaded, it's important to make sure they stand securely without the possibility of losing their balance if the driver has to step on the brakes. I prefer to drive by myself when transporting my horses, to make sure they are driven in the most considerate way possible, without a lot of needless braking or sudden acceleration. It's also important to take it easy when going around curves in the road, so they don't lose their balance. A horse that has been frightened in the trailer will always be a problem to travel with. Norway is a particularly difficult country for transporting horses because we have so many winding and hilly roads. It's

It is important to make sure the horse stands securely in the trailer. A horse that has been frightened in the trailer will always be a problem to travel with.

easier in countries with nice, straight freeways where you don't have to vary your speed as much.

As soon as the horses were securely situated in the trailer, we packed the last few things in the car and started the return journey. It took us nine hours this time too, and we didn't get home until late night. The stalls were ready for the horses, so luckily they were able to go right in and relax with some good food. It had been a long and educational trip for both of them, and I'm afraid it had been somewhat strenuous for poor little El Patron, although he quickly recovered when he got back home.

The next day we let him back out in the pasture, where he enjoyed the rest of his summer in peace and quiet with his friends.

During the fall months we didn't really do much with the yearlings other than daily care, some leisure walks and a short visit to the round pen now and then. The yearlings were in their own little pasture with other horses the same age, but after the summer pasture season was over they were moved in with Maikopchik, a new two-year old stallion that we had purchased in Holland. He was the new arrival in the stable, and therefore at the bottom of the pecking order. He spent some time with the other two-year olds at our stable, but sometimes their romping and playing got to be a little too much for him, so we let him go in with the yearlings instead. That worked very well. Nova and El Patron made it perfectly clear that they had no desire to challenge the new stallion. Horses will lower their necks, smack their lips and chew to show submission to another horse, and it's very rare for an older horse to pick on somebody who shows his or her own submission that clearly.

El Patron with the other yearlings.

THE TWO-YEAR-OLD

New Years Day came and went, and suddenly all of our horses were a year older. We were not in a hurry, however, when it came to the young horses. Some people probably think we do too little with our young horses, but that's a matter of preference. We start expecting more from the horses when they're two, at least when fall comes.

As spring approached we continued to work in the round pen. We didn't plan to enter El Patron in any show this season. In the spring we did some trail training and round pen practice in addition to daily routines. We put a bridle on him and had him stay in his stall with the bridle on while we put something good to eat in his tray. Other times he was outside running in the fields and playing with Nova, as well as a new playmate in the pasture. Qatana had her very last colt foal by Peleng. The foal was born right after the great animated movie "Spirit" came to the movie theaters, so choosing a name was easy this time. We thought Spirit was a name that suited him very well, since Peleng had passed away and he would also be Qatana's last foal. Spirit was the only yearling we had that spring, hence he got to be with the two who were a year older than he. That turned out very well. They got along nicely.

As we got closer to summer all three of them were placed in a stallion pasture together with a couple of other horses. There they got to stay and relax all summer and well into the fall.

In September we went to the annual Arabian auction in Holland, and by the time we got home it had really started to feel like fall. SR Nova had been sold over the summer, and the other stallions were brought in from summer pasture. Only El Patron and Spirit were left in the pasture. When we finally came for them, they were beside themselves with joy. They started neighing the moment they saw us, and seemed to be communicating to us that they didn't want to be left out in the pasture for another second. That wasn't so strange, actually. The field was pretty wet because it had rained heavily over the last few days. There was no doubt about it, the summer was over! There was only one thing on the horses' minds: to go with us and get into the warm, cozy stable again. As for us, we were ready to start working with our young horses again.

El Patron was two and a half by then, and we took him and his half-sister Anastacia to a class given by a Danish woman named Malene Kortsen. She specializes in Horsemanship and something she calls Passive Leadership. The whole point is for the horse to choose you as its leader.

We had taken classes in Horsemanship before, but this was a more attractive idea to me. I think it's important to find the method that suits you and your horse the best, and her method works perfectly for me.

Malene was only 22 years old, but had already gained a lot of experience with various methods of Natural Horsemanship. Her work and philosophy have a lot in common with Mark Rashid's (an internationally known trainer from Colorado). She teaches a philosophy that Mark has developed and teaches called "Passive Leadership," in which the human is a passive leader who doesn't dominate the horse or make it submissive and obedient by force. The goal is for the horse to choose you as its leader.

Malene is practicing the "friendship game" with El Patron.

Malene emphasized praising the horse for the things it does well instead of focusing on and punish the negative. Hence the training is an incredibly calm and pleasant time both for the horse and the leader. You don't see as much "waving" of ropes as you do in other forms of Horsemanship. With this method we actively use body language and invite the horse to join us.

This method allows individual horses to retain their different personalities That's actually one of the most important parts of this form of Natural Horsemanship. The horse is a horse, and we shouldn't change that. It shouldn't be an obedient machine that doesn't think for itself. It should be a horse with instincts, yet a horse who trusts its leader enough to follow him or her in any situation.

We started class on a Saturday morning with pouring rain. But since we had a new indoor arena it didn't matter what the weather threw at us. We started by playing six "games," which form the foundation for making the horse want to follow us.

Game 1: The Friendship Game

This game is about becoming good friends with your horse. The goal is to get the horse to accept touches anywhere on its body while it remains relaxed and calm.

You may think that sounds easy, but I'm telling you, it wasn't always easy for me to do, especially since I was dealing with a two-year-old stallion that was far

Standing on plastic.

more interested in his two-year-old half-sister who was in heat.

We had borrowed Natural Horsemanship halters for the occasion. They are designed to let the horse feel the pressure more softly and easily, and they have long ropes that make it possible to move all around the horse. These ropes are used for knocking on the horse to make it desensitized to the ropes, and in the end to feel unafraid of them.

This is a very important exercise. The rope is knocked against its tummy, under the legs, and basically everywhere on the horse's body.

Sometimes the instructor accidentally threw the rope a little too hard, making it smack into the side of the horse and scaring it more than she had intended. That made things a little harder for those of us who were just learning. My main problem, though, was hitting the horse in just the right spot. Admittedly, I cheated sometimes, only pretending to have done it all right. Otherwise I might still have been there, as I kept missing all the time! But I figured I'd get better at it with more time and practice.

When the horse is completely comfortable with these exercises, you can move on to the next game.

Game 2: Yield To Pressure

This is a preparation for riding the horse. The horse is supposed to yield to pressure on the halter, give in to the halter, or yield to a push by hand in the area where the leg aids are. We practiced bending the horse's head to both sides by lifting the rope a little, first to the right, then to the left, while we stood next to the horse's shoulder. To make the horse back up, we placed light pressure on the chest, and afterwards we turned the horse's head and made it turn around by placing light pressure in the leg aids area.

I was happy to discover that this game was easier for El Patron and me. It wasn't as hard to control the rope, or maybe I was just getting a little better at it by now. At least I didn't miss as much as before. Luckily most horses are very generous, so even if you do something wrong they'll forgive you as long as you're not being mean to them.

Game 3: Follow Me

The goal of this game is to make the horse follow its leader at the same speed as the leader and in the same direction, without going past the leader's shoulder and without stepping on the leader. The horse should stop when the leader stops. Body language is very important in this game. We learned to walk in a very distinctive way, so the horse would have no doubt which direction we were going in. We also had to show very clearly when we wanted to increase or decrease the speed. It was important to look in the direction we wanted to go, giving the horse a chance to see this. El Patron and I walked very determinedly around the riding arena. Sometimes my young stallion would get a little distracted when he was close to his half-sister, but I have to say I was very proud of him. In general he was incredibly good at concentrating and paying attention. After having walked around the riding arena for six hours, our shoes were filled with sand, our heads were spinning, and the horses, not to mention us two-legged creatures, were all but worn out.

El Patron feels safe with Malene.

Sunday was a good day. The sun was shining and we were outside in our new, big riding arena. We started the day with a little review of "The Friendship Game." Then we moved on to new games.

Game 4: Yield To Me and Come Closer To Me

This turned out to be my favorite game. It was a lot of fun! In this game you want the horse to back up when you look it in the eye, keep eye contact and point backward. As soon as the horse indicates a willingness to back up, you relax your posture and invite the horse to stand still. It was very effective and fun. El Patron caught on to the game quickly and was backing up like a champion. Afterwards we tried to make the horse come to us by inviting it toward us with body language. This also went really well for us. I added a little hand wave and El Patron instantly came at the slightest hand movement. Admittedly, I gave him a little treat or two while we were doing this game, so maybe that's why he excelled so quickly!

Game 5: Move Your Behind

In this game the horse is supposed to yield the rear part of its body while you have a chance to examine the middle muscle of the thigh and point at it.

This game was another success for El Patron. By now he and I were in harmony, and everything was working better between us. It was great, feeling our trust growing stronger and stronger with every new game. El Patron was a lot more confident, as was I. In addition I was much more aware of my own body language, so it was definitely a wonderful experience.

Game 6: Directing Your Horse Away From You

The horse should be tied to a relaxed line. You get it moving it in the direction you want it to go by using body language to show the way. That is, you lift your hand in the direction you are asking it to go. As your horse gets gradually better at this, you turn and use your body to signal for it to go in a different direction. This exercise is good for making your horse soft and nice. The exercise further prepares the horse for other exercises as well as for trailer training.

Again, this was a great exercise for El Patron. I found this to be an extremely fun and inspiring way to train. It felt as if I became more positive, calm and well balanced.

Once we finished the games, we took a break before going back to the indoor arena.

Malene had prepared a hurdle track with various challenges for the horses. We had to use everything we had learned in order to back up through hurdles, turn, walk through narrow passages, stand on a podium, walk on a tarp and rub the plastic all over the horse's body. All these exercises were designed to increase the horse's trust in humans (the leader) and reduce its anxiety about foreign objects.

All the horses that were participating in the class got through the exercises without any major problems. The prep work we had done throughout the course had made the horses accept us as their leaders, and they trusted that whatever we asked them to do was fully doable. It was an exciting and challenging experience, both for horses and leaders. For some horses – especially El Patron – this was so much fun that he even forgot about his interesting little half-sister for a few minutes. He was standing with all four legs on the podium, looking like he was receiving a gold medal at some sporting event!

The class was fun and very useful to everybody who participated. We learned so much in a very easygoing and quiet way, something that suited our Arabian horses very well. Many of the exercises were nicely tailored to young horses that are being prepped for riding, and we benefited greatly in that regard.

Since we had Malene visiting with us, we took advantage of the opportunity to go a few extra steps with both El Patron and Anastacia. The day after classes were over, we took El Patron with us into the round pen. Even though we had not worked in the round pen during classes, only with the horse on a line, it was now time for a little "join-up." El Patron walked calmly around in a circle, and then he was supposed to come when Malene called him. This is a good way to train the horse to concentrate. It didn't take more than a few rounds before El Patron understood what he was supposed to do.

We brought the saddle and saddle blanket and put them both on the ground. El Patron was then given a chance to sniff the items and get familiar with them while they were lying on the ground. After he examined them thoroughly, Malene put the blanket on his back. Some

Checking out the saddle for the first time.

Preparing to put the saddle on for the first time.

horses will react badly to a thing like that, and if so you have to be patient and wait until the horse is more comfortable with the situation before you proceed. El Patron is actually an incredibly easygoing and trusting horse, and the introduction to a saddle and saddle blanket wasn't a problem at all. After the saddle blanket had been off and on a few times, we put the saddle on him, too.

At first we just put it loosely on top of his back before we took it off again. But after a while we had to tighten the girth. When you do that it is essential that

you make sure the saddle is sitting correctly on the horse's back. It has to be tight enough that it can't swing around, because if it does, you risk ruining the horse's feeling of security.

The saddle was put in place and tightened, and then came the reaction! El Patron took off like a bucking bronco. He jumped and bounced and twisted, but the saddle stayed put as if it was glued to him. Malene thought it was fine to let the horse buck like this. In her opinion it was better to let the horse test it out properly, and to release his body

El Patron is bucking to get rid of the saddle, but he calms down after a little while.

tension. After a few rounds he calmed down, and then we had to let him run the other way for a while too.

Horses need to try everything out on both sides, so it was necessary to let him keep the saddle on while he ran the other way as well. And sure enough – he made the same leaps and bounds this time, but maybe not quite as many as he had in the first direction.

It didn't take long before El Patron was trotting calmly around the arena, looking like he had been doing this his whole life. Then we stopped him and took the saddle off, giving him a chance to rest.

We didn't put the saddle on any more that day. The remaining work was done without a saddle.

After the break, Malene got out some boxes to stand on in order to get the horse used to her being taller than he. She leaned over the horse, lifting her arms over his head. El Patron didn't care about any of this, as he had been trained like this when he was little. The reason we kept lifting our arms above his head was to train him to not get scared when something approached him from behind. Again Malene did the exercise from both sides of the horse. Afterwards we took it a step further. As I held him by the lead rope, Malene was lifted onto his back. First she lay down on her side, and then she brought her leg over his back, but she didn't sit up. She only let herself slide gently down on the other side of him. We did this a few times from right to left, with Malene never sitting up completely. El Patron was still

The first time El Patron has someone on his back.

The Horse's Blind Spots:
For one arm length in front of the head, the horse cannot see its leader. Nor can it see anything right behind its buttock. Right above the back is another blind spot.

totally calm. He was not afraid despite all the strange things we were doing to him. After all the exciting work over the last weekend nothing seemed to surprise him anymore. When Malene realized that he accepted having her on his back, she sat up with a straight back before getting off on the other side. Finally she got up on his back while I led him around the round pen. El Patron was still totally calm. None of the exercises had scared him, and he had been receiving tons of rewards and positive feedback. After one last round on both the right and the left side, we quit, well satisfied that El Patron had taken his very first important step toward his life as a riding horse.

The next day we saddled El Patron and sat on him again, getting up and down a few times. That was the end of the course for the time being, and El Patron was free for a while to give all the new things he had learned a chance to sink in.

El Patron accepts his rider.

THE HORSE'S ZONES

Zone 1
The horse is driven backwards by pressure.

Zone 2:
The horse's shoulder is pushed away by pressure (the whole horse is moved in this way).

Zone 3:
Passive zone belongs to the leg aids.

Zone 4:
The horse's behind is pushed away by pressure.

Zone 5:
The horse is pushed forward by pressure.

When we place pressure on the horse and it reacts the way it's supposed to, we reward it by relieving the pressure as soon as it tries.

THE THREE-YEAR-OLD

We had a great winter with a lot of nice weather. After El Patron was familiar with the saddle, rider and bridle, he didn't have any further training, but was allowed to be a colt for a while longer. He spent a lot of time outside playing with Spirit. They were having a ball together! Neither of them had been shoed yet, which was an advantage when the snow came. Snow has a tendency to accumulate in clumps under the hooves of a shoed horse.

In areas where the snow stays on the ground for a long time, it's a good idea to use frost nails on a shoed horse. Frost nails are temporary, and are used to help horses keep their footing on icy ground. Around here the snow melts quickly, so we use frost nails only if the horse is to be ridden every day. Frost nails can be troublesome for young horses, as they can easily step on themselves, causing leg injuries.

El Patron grew steadily throughout the winter. It was hard to believe that he was already three years old! His first challenge as a three-year-old was a certification event. Here in Norway Arabian horses are not certified for breeding until the year they are three-year-olds. The requirement for the young horses is to have passed a lunging test. They also have to be inspected and evaluated by the judges and have a thorough veterinarian exam.

Even with all the experience we've had with such certification events, it's not always easy to get the colt to behave properly. It should be easy to handle, and it should be able to perform the walk, trot and gallop on the lunge line without side-reins.

Of course, we had brought El Patron to a show once before, but a certification event isn't quite the same thing. It can easily turn into a tense affair when so many different stallions, young and old, are gathered in the same place.

We were optimistic, however, as we started training El Patron to get him ready for the event. Point one on the program was lunging. Whenever I start working with a young horse, I prefer to use saddle, bridle and side-reins during lunging practice. That way the horse has more balance and it gets used to both the saddle and the bridle at the same time.

The first few times I made the side-reins pretty long, but as El Patron gradually got more used to having something in his mouth, I tightened them so that he got a more correct collection, working nicely with the reins. When the horse walks calmly and obediently on the bit, it also builds the right muscles. But it isn't easy to get the horse to walk in a balanced way without the side-reins. Young horses aren't always able to relax and concentrate on what they're supposed to do when there's a lot of activity going on around them. I think it's a lot easier when you have side-reins on, especially with horses that are naturally a little uneasy. We didn't really have much of a problem with El Patron. He had grown into an exceptionally well-balanced and harmonious colt.

Another part of the preparations was shoeing. We had already made an appointment with a farrier who we knew was easy-going and would take his time. You never know beforehand how the horse will react the first time it gets shoed, hence patience is very important. Previously the farrier had only been there to rasp El Patron's hooves a little, so we weren't sure how this would turn out.

We always make one of us is present when the farrier visits. It's good to be standing in front of the horse and helping out in case there are problems. Sometimes the younger horses also need a little support from the side. Not all of them think it's an easy thing to stand still on three legs – at least not for any length of time.

If the horse is a little nervous and afraid, we often decide to start it out with shoes only on the forelegs. That way it doesn't have to stand still as long. In such cases it might also be a good idea to have a few treats on hand, so the horse gets rewarded for being good. As mentioned earlier, I'm usually not too keen on handing out treats. Normally I just praise and pat the horse and leave it at that. But in this particular potentially stressful situation I think it's all right to offer a little extra reward.

El Patron, however, gave us no reason to worry. The treats remained in my pocket. He was really good throughout the entire shoeing process, making no fuss at all. Toward the end he started getting a little tired of it all, but he still stood still until the farrier was done. At that point we literally showered him with praise and pats!

PS: After the horse has been shoed, it is important to remove leftovers of the shoeing process – for instance clippings and old seams. If these are not removed right away, other horses may step on them and get them wedged into their hooves. That would both hurt and cause infection of the hoof. You should therefore take care to find all sharp scraps and throw them away in the trash.

El Patron had brand new shoes and was ready for more training. In order to have some variety, we spent time in the round pen, both with and without a saddle. I made sure to lunge him in the round pen too. The ground is heavier than in a regular arena, so this gives the horse a nice break and helps it to build muscle and strength.

We also started sitting on El Patron's back briefly, to keep him from getting bored with too much one-sided training. The smallest and lightest rider at the stable had the honor of riding El Patron in the beginning, while I had him on the lunge line. He didn't react to having a rider on his back again. After just a couple of training sessions, I was able to let him off the lunge line. He was walking nicely and calmly around the riding arena, as if having a person on his back was the most natural thing in the world to him.

Unexpected things can happen, however, even with a calm colt like El Patron. One day when we were training in the indoor arena, I noticed that he seemed a little tense. But he was walking nicely so I didn't think any more of it. That was a mistake! Usually I stop training when I notice that something isn't quite right, but this time I failed to heed the warning signs, maybe because I was so used to El Patron never getting upset about anything. I don't really know what it was that scared him, but suddenly he jumped and bucked, causing the saddle to get out of whack. And that's all it took. El Patron totally lost it and started bucking and thrashing like a rodeo horse. The poor girl who was riding him landed on the ground with a thump. Luckily she didn't get hurt. As for El Patron, he continued to jump and bounce with the saddle all askew. We finally managed to rein him in and fix the saddle. The rider climbed back up while I held my breath. What would happen next? But it seemed that El Patron was over the scare. Well, almost over it, at least. He still seemed a little tense and unsure, so we didn't take any chances. We had him on the lunge line for the rest of the session. We certainly didn't want any more surprises!

The first few times a horse walks with a rider on its back, it may look a little unsteady and indecisive. The weight on its back changes its center of balance, so walking is different from what it's used to. You can easily see this on shorter horses that have long legs. They have more problems finding their balance with a rider than a more rectangular horse does. One of the important parts of the training process is riding them with their body as straight as possible, so they can find their natural balance again.

When we felt that his training was reasonably under control, it was time for some "beauty treatment." We wanted El Patron to look his very best for the Certification event. In the end, we decided not to clip him, but to show him in his winter coat. Before taking him to his first show as a yearling, we had shaved him. But the Certification event was taking place so early in the year that it was still pretty cold outside. Without his warm winter coat, we ran the risk of having El Patron get too chilled. We could of course have used a cover on him and kept him warm that way, but Arabians have a very thin, fine layer of skin, and can get sores from the rubbing of a cover if it's not sitting just right.

At a horse certification event like the ones we have there is one thing that counts just as much if not more as the horse's behavior, and that is for the horse to be properly sound. This means it should be fit and healthy, and look like it too. It's therefore important that young horses are fed correctly, helping them grow up to be healthy, beautiful horses.

The feed we use is a special feed from Germany (St Hippolyt). They have a formula for foals and young horses, as well as a special formula for Arabians. El Patron had been getting this feed for quite a while, and before the certification we gave him a little extra energy feed (Struktur E) too. This is a feed that for several years has been voted Best of Europe, hence we felt pretty sure that our horses were getting all the nutrients they should have. In addition to the energy feed, El Patron was also getting a vitamin and mineral supplement that had been recommended to us by German nutritional experts. The mixture was called Mikro Vital and contained extra minerals.

As the time approached we felt we had done everything in our power to prepare El Patron for the Certification event. What could possibly go wrong? Well, quite a few things, as it turned out...

El Patron is now three years old, and has lots of fun running in the snow.

CERTIFICATION DAY

The big Certification day finally arrived. The event itself took place at Rine's farm, so we were actually on home ground. The advantage of that was of course that El Patron knew the surroundings. However, at the same time things weren't normal. There were unfamiliar horses all over the place, and a hustle and bustle of strange sounds and smells everywhere.

A lot of different horses were coming for certification: pony breeds, Arabians and riding horses. Each group was to be tested differently. The ponies were to be harnessed and shown in a carriage. The riding horses were to be shown in free jumping and riding tests. The Arabians were to have a riding test or a lunging test.

El Patron behaved perfectly during the vet exam. I hadn't been too sure how he would handle this exam, but El Patron stood there like a shining light while the vet examined him. Afterwards he was measured, and that also went just fine. I started relaxing, thinking this was all going to be a breeze.

Then came the big moment: the lunging test. Don't even ask! El Patron seemed to have forgotten everything he had learned, and then some. As I started warming him up before our turn, I realized that he was suddenly impossible to communicate with. All he cared about was making contact with all those great-looking stallions all around him, and he was neighing and calling to everyone he saw. When it came time for us to go into the arena I was already dripping with sweat. And things only got worse. Inside the arena he continued to ignore my desperate attempts at communicating with him. I might as well have saved my strength. To El Patron the only ones who mattered were the other stallions – certainly not his boring, old owner!

All right, to be totally honest, I guess I'll have to accept some of the blame for El Patron's unruly and unfocussed behavior. I always get really nervous and tense before a Certification event, and of course this affects the horse too and makes things worse.

After the lunging test, El Patron was inspected and then we were done. It was a great relief to have it be over. But the feeling of relief didn't last long. Next came the anxious waiting for the results. Would he pass or not? After what seemed like an eternity, we got the results. El Patron was certified for breeding, and we could take a deep breath of relief after a long and hard day.

But of course, the day wasn't over yet. Regardless of how tired we were, 25 horses were waiting impatiently for their evening meal. I was completely drained by the time we finally said goodnight to the horses. It's extra hard to be both an organizer and a participant of such an event, and my bed felt particularly good that night!

65

El Patron on his Certification day.

SHOWING

It's a good thing we humans tend to forget quickly all the stress we sometimes bring on ourselves. We like to remember only the pleasant things. It shouldn't come as a big surprise, then, to find out who signed up to help organize and host the 1st of May Horse Show - me. (You know, some people just never learn!) Showing your horse at a horse show, however, is very different from showing your horse at a certification event. I definitely prefer a show. At horse shows you have international judges, there's music, and you're allowed to bring a helper with you into the ring. I could have used a helper during the Certification event!

During the time leading up to the show we continued our training in the same manner as before. We had also arranged for a handler who would be showing the horse for us. His name was Kjetil, and prior to the show he came to the stable to train El Patron. Our young colt needed a little refresher course on how to run nicely on a lead rope next to the handler. The whole point of this is for the horse to show off, preferably by putting on a little show. The more it prances around with its tail in the air, the better it is. Unfortunately, showing off is not one of El Patron's strengths. He is a little too even-keeled and easygoing. Of course, on an everyday basis that's exactly what you want, a stable and reliable horse, but when it comes to the show ring it's more fun when they blow air through their noses and look a little wild and spunky.

Kjetil worked very hard to get El Patron a little more "on edge." Sometimes he succeeded, and I was very impressed when the horse trotted off with his tail

gloriously in the air. We started nurturing a tiny little hope that maybe it wasn't impossible to turn El Patron into a real show horse after all!

As the show day was approaching we decided to shave El Patron. A horse's head looks a little nobler and prettier when you remove its long winter coat.

When you're planning to cut your horse's coat, it's important to time it well with the day of the show. Dapples, horses with mottled or spotted markings, may be cut just about any day up to the day before the show. But when it comes to horses with bay and chestnut or sorrel coat colors, they should not be cut any later than six weeks prior to the show, or else you remove their beautiful color. Chestnut or sorrel horses get a different reddish tone that is more muted and not as pretty when it has just been cut. The same thing happens to bay and black horses, while those that are white or gray will still look clean and pretty.

The show day arrived with beautiful weather. The sun greeted us from a clear, blue sky, with no wind and a pleasant 68-degree Fahrenheit temperature. I'm afraid those of us who live in a country like Norway, with a very extreme climate, get almost obsessively concerned with the weather. We're always afraid that the weather might completely torpedo our big events, with rain and wind and even worse. Hence the beautiful weather helped a lot to make the day so successful. Horses, exhibitors and judges were beaming along with the sun, and we even had to dig out some sunscreen for the judges. Even so, they were pretty red in the cheeks after judging out in the arena for several hours. There was even one who could have competed with a certain Rudolph over who had the reddest nose!

Kjetil showing El Patron in the ring.

El Patron and Kjetil did a great job in the ring. As a matter of fact, El Patron ended up placing first in his class. We were so proud of him! Afterwards the winners of each class had to compete for the Champion titles. El Patron did well again, showing off his best side, but unfortunately he still didn't quite make it to the top. A horse named Zamir beat him to the title. Zamir was a one-year-old colt from our stud stallion, Pinczow. Even though I was rooting for El Patron, I had to admit that Zamir, with his beautiful head and movements, deserved to win. We were plenty satisfied with El Patron taking home the Reserve Champion title and thought that wasn't bad at all.

The next day there was a riding competition. Again we had beautiful weather, and Rine greeted me with good news. She told me we had gotten a new colt foal from Qatana and Pinczow the night before, which meant El Patron had a new half-brother . This news put us in the same high spirits as the day before. I literally walked around humming to myself, thinking that life couldn't be any better, blissfully ignorant of the bad news waiting right around the corner...

After the Dutch judge had finished judging the riding classes, I asked her if she wanted to join me for a walk out to the pasture to look at our mares. I didn't react to the fact that Asmena was lying down out there, because she often enjoyed relaxing like that in nice, warm weather. But when we got closer, I saw something lying on the ground next to her, and my heart almost stopped. It was a dead foal.

Asmena, who had a month yet to go of her pregnancy, had aborted her foal. Something had obviously gone terribly wrong. I stood there looking down at the foal with a big lump in my throat. It was so pretty – a tiny, little chestnut filly foal with one of the most beautiful heads I've ever seen. It had a thin, little blaze and two white socks on its legs.

It was so sad. I felt like sitting right down and crying. Especially since this happened to Asmena's foal. She had been having problems getting pregnant, and hadn't had a foal in years. It was a great joy to us when she finally succeeded. But now there wouldn't be a foal after all. When you work with horses, you'll find there are few steps between happiness and sadness. One moment we were so delighted about Qatana's foal, and then, only a few hours later, we were standing there with grief in our hearts, looking at this tiny, beautiful animal that wouldn't get a chance to grow up.

NEW CHALLENGES

Life moves on, and luckily there are more joys than sorrows. El Patron was in the process of becoming a fine, adult horse, that was going to be tried for the first time as a stallion at stud. The mares that were to be covered at our stud had started arriving. We decided that El Patron would cover SR Amia, who was an offspring from Pinczow and Asmena, in other words a full sister of the foal we lost at the beginning of May.

It's always a big deal when a young stallion is to cover a mare for the first time. Enthusiasm is usually not a problem, but they don't always get it right at first. It was actually pretty funny to watch El Patron. He was so much like his father. Just as Peleng used to do, he neighed and talked to the mare, almost before he was out of the stable. He was eager, but when he came closer to the mare he suddenly had all the time in the world to sniff and check her out. Pinczow, on the other hand, had no time for chitchat. He went straight to work – no dawdling with that guy.

We had two very different stallions to deal with this season. One "gentleman" who liked to flirt, and one "bulldozer" who just wanted to get the job done. As for the mares, it varies from one to the other what type of stallion they prefer. In some cases the mares get tired of too much "chatting," while others seem to like having a little time to say hello to the stallion and get familiar with him before covering.

El Patron smells the mare.

El Patron had a little trouble his first time. Amia is a big mare, but he eventually figured it out. After Amia came Minella, a horse from another farm. Minella was smaller than Amia, and a full-grown and experienced mare, so the covering went much smoother with her.

After that we just had to wait and see. Were the mares pregnant, or not? It turned out that Minella was in foal, and for a while we thought the same about Amia, because she didn't go into heat again. But later in the fall we realized that she had either aborted or absorbed the egg. This can easily happen when the mare is not very far along, and sometimes it's hard for them to go in heat again afterwards.

Training El Patron.

In between coverings El Patron kept training as he had before, with a little riding and lunging. We don't really train the horses very hard on the days that they're covering. It's hard work for the stallions, and it requires them to use a set of totally different muscles than they normally do. On days when no training or covering was going on, El Patron was in the paddock. The idea was to have him relax there, but that didn't really work out. He had to share a paddock with Pinczow because all the other fields were taken.

The two stallions were taking turns outside in the paddock for half a day each. Since they regarded each other as rivals, however, this caused a lot of frustration. Every time one of them went into the paddock, it seemed the other one had been there and marked his territory (which means they urinated in different spots around the paddock to indicate the areas belonged to them). That meant of course that the other one had to go and mark all the same places where the previous stallion had been. When this ritual was finished, they would start neighing at the mares that were walking around on the other side of the fence. You wouldn't say there was much relaxing going on, that's for sure!

The noise spread to the stable as well. Fortunately we didn't have too many horses inside at this time, but the constant rivalry between the two stallions definitely got to be tiring after a while. They even started to lose weight. They were scowling at each other every time covering was going on, probably just wishing the other one would get lost. This rivalry seemed to be harder on Pinczow. He was the oldest, and had for all practical purposes been the king of the stable for many years. He was not at all happy about this eager "crown prince" who had started challenging his territory.

Vivian A. Harrison, the dressage rider,
training El Patron .

After the summer was over, and the other horses started coming in from summer pasture, El Patron moved into his stall in the barn. We had a small, separate compartment for the colts. SR Armani, who was four, occupied the biggest stall. The stall between El Patron and Armani was occupied by SR Prakash, a one-year-old colt. He didn't cause any trouble and had a calming effect on the two older colts. Those two would probably have liked nothing better than to test their strength in a real fight had they been given the chance.

The stable became more peaceful once we got El Patron away from the mares. He's a stallion who talks a lot, and that can be a little tiresome for the other horses, but it's kind of entertaining too. He'll always whinny when we come into the stable and say something to him. He answers and looks at us with those big, kindly eyes of his. Most people simply melt when they see how adorable he is. He can carry on long conversations with people who come into the stable, Whinnying and neighing and whinnying again. As long as you keep eye contact with him and say something, he'll answer you back. He is simply wonderful!

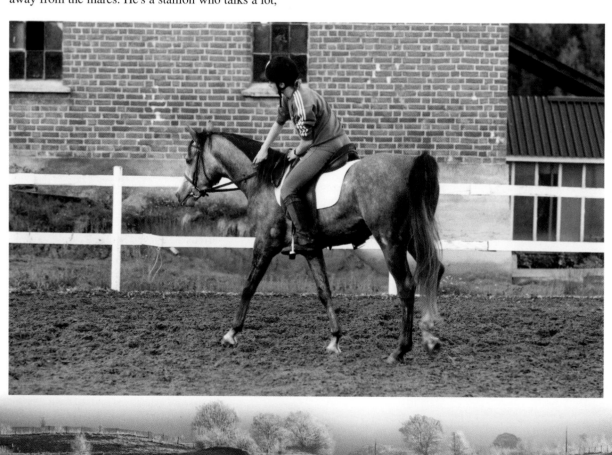

A DIFFICULT CHOICE

We were very happy with El Patron's progress, and had had a lot of positive experiences with him and the other horses throughout the summer. Hence, spirits were high at our stud farm. But this good feeling didn't last too long. When fall came, the problems started. Asmena and Qatana, who were our oldest broodmares, had been going downhill for some time. By now we were wondering if we should put an end to their suffering.

Asmena was the first Russian mare Rine had bought. She suffered from a shoulder injury which she had had since she was a yearling. In addition, she had been having some problems with her hind legs after she lost her foal, Yet I think she had had a nice summer. She had been able to go outside, move around freely, and lie down in the field where there was plenty of room to rest. Winter, however, was a different story. In previous winters she'd gotten stiff and sore and was clearly miserable. Was it right for us to make her suffer through yet another winter? I think we already knew the answer, but we didn't want to admit it. Asmena was the gentlest creature you could imagine. When she looked at us with her beautiful, brown eyes, it wasn't easy to be a horse owner and have to decide whether or not to end her life.

Qatana, El Patron's mother, was not well either. She was suffering from a stiff hind leg, and we had a hard time keeping her weight up when she was in the field with her foals. This time she actually stayed pretty healthy for quite a while after foaling, but later in the fall she started shedding pounds very drastically. She also got some eczema on her back, and was looking pretty run-down overall.

We tried taking Qatana inside and giving her more food. That didn't help. The other horses were still in the pasture, and Qatana, who had always been such a quiet and collected mare, didn't like having to be inside when the others were outside. It didn't matter to her that she was getting extra good food. She kept pacing around her stall, constantly pushing herself against the door until she had rubbed her neck raw. We were forced to let her go outside with the others again, without her having eaten her food. Then we tried feeding her a little extra out in the pasture, but Qatana ate so slowly that she didn't manage to get enough nourishment out there, either.

Finally we decided that we had to wean her foal, because this couldn't continue. Qatana was placed in the stall next to the foal so the weaning process would cause as little stress as possible. Even so it turned into the most troublesome weaning process we had ever witnessed. Qatana was pacing around her stall again, getting thinner and thinner each day. Finally we let her go outside with the other mares, while the foal remained in its stall. She actually calmed down faster out there with her friends. But we realized that we definitely could not take the chance of letting Qatana have any more foals, considering how bad she was this time.

We did some serious soul searching before we eventually made a final and very difficult decision. Asmena and Qatana would go to the eternal fields in a dignified way. As hard as this decision was, we felt it was the only right thing to do at this point.

Next we called several veterinarians to find out how to get this done in the most humane way possible. One thing we were absolutely sure of: they were not going to be transported to any slaughterhouse and end their

days there. These two great mares would be allowed to go to their final rest at home.

The day we had chosen came with glorious, sunny weather. The stud farm was bathed in the most beautiful light under a clear, blue sky, but even the nicest weather in the world couldn't have made this anything but a very sad and difficult day. I woke up with a lump in my throat, and I was pacing in circles myself while we waited for the vet to come. When I saw his car drive into the farmyard, I felt downright sick. It was time to get the mares.

Those few steps out to the field were the heaviest steps I have ever taken as a horse owner. Qatana looked at me with her big, beautiful eyes. It felt as if she could see right into my soul and knew what I was going to do. She came willingly, and my tears ran freely as I walked her to the chosen spot outside the stable. I had mixed up a bucket of good, warm porridge – her favorite food – and as she ate it, she was sedated. Afterwards the vet gave the shots, and within a few seconds she collapsed. I just sat there, stroking her face and seeing the gentle, kind light of her eyes go out.

Then I had to repeat the same steps for Asmena. She came just as willingly and trustingly as Qatana had, which didn't make the task any easier for me. Asmena got the same, good porridge, and within minutes she had taken her least breath as well. Then I just sat there, thinking of all the wonderful moments we had had together and of all the beautiful foals these two mares had given us.

I felt so utterly sad. Not only were our two greatest broodmares gone forever, but a chapter of our lives as breeders had also passed. We had lost the last two ancestral mares that had helped lay the foundation of our entire breeding program. Now they were gone, all four great ones. Asmena, who had been the first broodmare, Primanka who had been the second, Qatana the third, and not the least Peleng, our wonderful stallion who had been the pillar of our breeding program.

We still had Pinczow, the king of our stable. I truly hoped that he would be able to continue as both a stallion at stud and a riding horse for many years to come.

There were many strange thoughts going through my mind that fall day. Even as the grief and sorrow sat like a painful knot in my stomach, I felt in many ways relieved to have it over with. After the mares had been put down and the truck had taken them away, we took some time to wipe our tears before getting started on our work in the stable again. After a while life felt a little lighter again. The horses had to be taken outside, there was mucking to do and also training. It also helped that both Rine and I were totally convinced that this was the best thing for our two old mares. They left our world in a dignified way.

But a chapter was irrevocably at its end. Now it was up to the younger mares and stallions to take over and continue their bloodline into the future.

Asmena is old and sick.

Qatana as we like to remember her.

THE ROAD CONTINUES

El Patron looked like he enjoyed all the new challenges we threw at him, and we grew increasingly fond of our easy-going, gentle stallion. Since the day he was born he has pretty much only given us joy. He's a wonderful horse with a great temper, and continues to talk to everyone who cares to listen.

Inside the stall he was careful with those who were littler than he, and there was never any tendency toward nipping or biting. El Patron has been a very easy horse to work with, and together we've learned a lot. It is extremely educational to work with horses. Every day we learn something new.

We hope El Patron has a long and exciting life as a stallion ahead of him, bringing joy to not only us, but to all the new friends, two-legged as well as four, that he will meet along the way.

All horses are different, of course. Not all of them are as easy to handle as El Patron. It is very, very rewarding, however, once you manage to get close to these beautiful creatures and feel that you can really communicate with them. When the horse manages to tell you something through its body language, you know that you're on the right track. Many horses are very good at using their bodies to express themselves, to tell you that something is bothering them, for instance. Keep your eyes and heart open to your horse, and you'll go far in your friendship with your animal.

I have made plenty of mistakes along the way, and will probably make many more. But horses have big hearts.

They will happily forgive you as long as you treat them fairly. I tend to talk to my horses a lot. I notice that it helps me concentrate more on what I'm doing. It also helps me see what I need to do, and then I try to pass this thought on to the horse. Horses are extremely telepathic, and if you manage to stay focused and calm, it's unbelievable how much you can sometimes get the horse to understand.

When you work with horses, it is important to realize that your relationship should be a partnership. The horse and its rider should work together. That's why it doesn't work very well if you try to force the horse into submission. Rather, you should try to make the work a pleasure for both you and the horse. If the horse isn't happy, you are not going to achieve the best results.

Even so, it's essential that you don't let a young horse beat you in situations where the horse is actively trying to compete for power. You are the one who makes decisions. It's usually young horses that tend to test limits the most. In my experience mares are usually easier in this respect, although they may have assertive tendencies, which you have to learn to deal with. I'd therefore recommend for everyone to get a qualified professional to "break in" their horses for riding; somebody who's good at staying on the horse's case.

I like horses that have distinct personalities and horses that "answer" you; by that I mean the ones who manage to express how they feel about the things I'm doing. I have seen many distinct personalities in horses we've worked with at the stud farm.

You can achieve a new kind of relationship and contact with horses, especially when you start riding and work more intensely with them. We have horses with senses

Vivian Harrison riding El Patron at their first dressage show. They became Club Champions!

of humor, and horses that are good workers. Some are lazy, and if they were humans, they would probably hang out at the nearest junk food joint, eating hamburgers all day. Don't be afraid to see the humorous aspects of your horse and foster its unique personality.

Remember also to take your time in everything you do. If the horse doesn't understand what you want, don't lose patience, but try again. Hurry slowly, as I like to say, and take a step back rather than a big jump forward. Be aware that horses live for 25 to 30 years, and it's our responsibility to make sure they get the right training and become easy to deal with. A horse like that will usually have a good life with somebody who loves it more than anything on Earth. Problem horses, however, will have a much more difficult life and will often be shuffled from one owner to the next. It is a big responsibility for us, the breeders, to breed sound and healthy animals with even temperaments. Later, it's up to the owners to care for these horses, with their unique personalities.

We've had our dreams come true by getting to work with horses. Therefore we want our horses to fulfill the dreams of other people as well. If we can manage that, we've achieved a lot as breeders.

Good luck to those of you who dream of some day owning your own horse, and to those of you whose dreams have already come true!

Epilogue

El Patron is now well on his way to more advanced training. He started in his first endurance event when he was four. In the spring of the year he turned five, he got his final breeding certificate. After that he was showing off on the dressage course. He became club champion in dressage at his first show! Later on he won several dressage shows and has also placed high in other shows.

He has started his show-jumping training and he loves it! It's not unusual to see him bucking happily after clearing a jump. Fun for him, not quite as much fun for the rider!

El Patron still gives us lots of joy and happy moments every day – and best of all – he's still at the start of his career!

Thanks to everyone who's helped him become a great riding horse:
Silje Hove, who was responsible for him during his youth; Hilde Søndervik who helped out as a test rider; Line Hamre who rode El Patron in style at Kongsberg; Odd Willy Berg who took care of El Patron and rode dressage while we were away on vacation; Vivian Harrison who taught El Patron a variety of dressage movements and who also rode him at dressage shows; Mette Eltervåg who started endurance riding with him; Ulrikke Lindal who took El Patron hiking, and last but not least; Mari Myrebøe who accepted the challenge of starting show-jumping with El Patron.

We are sure El Patron will bring us lots of joy in the future.